T*A*C*K Secret Service

Created by MARVIN MILLER

Written by NANCY K. ROBINSON

Illustrated by Alan Tiegreen

SCHOLASTIC BOOK SERVICES

NEW YORK • TORONTO • LONDON • AUCKLAND • SYDNEY • TOKYO

For my wife Matty—with love always,
M. M.

To my dear and daring friend,
Steven Scher—
N. K. R.

ISBN 0-590-32404-7

12 11 10 9 8 7 6 5 4 3 2 1 10 2 3 4 5 6/8
Printed in the U.S.A. 21

CONTENTS

SANDY HARBOR, WEDNESDAY, DECEMBER 13—

T*A*C*K is a network of kids. It is not a club. We do not have regular meetings in a clubhouse or anything like that. We do not wear buttons or T-shirts with T*A*C*K written across them.

No one knows about T*A*C*K. We work undercover. Our job is to serve people in the town of Sandy Harbor. We are a secret service.

Let me give you a quick rundown of the T*A*C*K team. The letters stand for our names:

T* for Toria.

That's me. My name is Victoria Gardner, but please call me Toria. I do not answer to Vicky. I am the one writing this journal. No one told me to do it. I just need the practice. You see, I am planning to be a newspaper reporter when I grow up.

A* for Abby.

Abigail Pinkwater is my best friend. Abby moved away last year, but I'd rather not talk about it. Abby is an honorary member of T*A*C*K. She is also our Agent-on-Remote which means "at a distance."

C* stands for Chuck.

Chuck is a trusted member of the T*A*C*K team. He is one of those people you can always count on.

K* is the code name for Will Roberts.

Will is the only one with a code name. Will is special. He is our leader, but he wouldn't want me to say that. Besides, in a funny way, we are all equal in T*A*C*K.

Will's code name comes from Morse code. In Morse code "K" is dash, dot, dash (– · –). This signal was used in early telegraph language to mean "Switch." SWITCH TO SEND or GO AHEAD, I'M LISTENING . . .

Will's mind works like a switch. It switches all over the place. He is also a very good listener. He doesn't just listen; he *hears*!

Sometimes Will Roberts hears too well. He gets into trouble. One time our teacher, Miss Miller, asked Will to divide the number eight in half. Right away Will had three answers: four, two zeros, and two threes (one of them backwards).

He showed Miss Miller:

$$8 \div 2 = 4$$

8 = 0 0

8 = Ɛ3

Miss Miller thought he was being fresh. He wasn't. Will Roberts just thinks that way. That is why he is so valuable to T*A*C*K .

Most of our cases are just mysteries, everyday problems and matters of life and death. We don't usually get mixed up in spying or intrigue. But, last Saturday, at an innocent Science Fair, the T*A*C*K team suddenly found itself in the middle of OPERATION GOLDFISH!

This is what happened . . .

*T*A*C*K Secret Service: Operation Goldfish*

SANDY HARBOR, SATURDAY, DECEMBER 9—

I walked into our school gymnasium carrying my science exhibit in a cardboard box. Today is the annual Science Fair. Kids from every school in the district will be here.

Yesterday our science teacher, Mr. Molinaro, told us to come early. "Try to get there before those kids from Monrose Elementary arrive. Some of them are a bit clumsy, but I'm sure they mean well."

Monrose kids do *not* mean well. Last year a kid named Red Jamieson aimed right for my table and knocked over my model of a solar house.

This year I have another solar house—a later model.

"Hi, Toria," Rachel said. I stopped and looked at her exhibit. It was a solar house. I sighed. There will probably be at least fifty solar houses at the fair this year.

I moved on to look at the next table.

"Growing mold on bread?" I asked Emily.

Emily nodded.

Will Roberts was at the last table in the row. Will was wearing his best green-and-blue plaid shirt. It wasn't as faded as his other shirts. Will has five shirts. They are all exactly alike. Will says he just happens to enjoy that plaid.

"Hi, Will," I said. "Where's your volcano?"

"Broke," Will said. "Erupted in the kitchen last night."

"Ick!" I said when I saw what was lying on his table. "Now *your* moldy bread really looks moldy."

Will looked up. "This is not mold, Toria," he said. "This is slime. This slime is similar to conditions that exist on the planet Mars. I am growing food on Mars."

"Oh." I felt bad. I hadn't meant to hurt Will's feelings.

"Wait a minute!" Will suddenly reached over the slime and grabbed my arm. He whispered,

"This isn't a real exhibit. It's a *cover*!"

"A what?" I set my solar house down.

"A cover! A fake! I just want to be able to keep an eye on Hugo's exhibit. Listen, Toria . . . " Will lowered his voice. I could hardly hear him. "Hugo's plans are missing—the plans for his science exhibit! Someone took them right out of his knapsack yesterday. And it just so happens that Red Jamieson and his friend Lester were hanging around our school yesterday."

"You're kidding!" I looked over at Hugo. Hugo Small is the most brilliant kid at our school. He was busy connecting a coil and some wires from a telephone to a little black box. There was a bowl of real goldfish on the table.

"What is it?" I asked Hugo.

Hugo blinked. "Do you really want to see?" he asked shyly.

"I want to see too!" Rachel called. She came running over. Rachel is quite nosy.

Hugo cleared his throat. "Now, let's say you are away from home and you want to feed your goldfish. You can feed them by telephone. You see—"

Rachel interrupted. "All right, so you call

your goldfish on the telephone. Then what do you say?"

"Er . . . no, Rachel," Hugo said. "You see—"

"—and, besides," Rachel went on, "what if your goldfish don't know where you put their food?"

"Um . . . Rachel," Hugo said politely. "You don't talk to your goldfish on the telephone." Hugo pushed a button on the phone. The phone rang.

"The ring of the phone sets off a device that automatically releases a tiny bit of food into the goldfish bowl. But not every ring sets off the device. If it did, the goldfish would be fed every time someone called your house. They would get sick. Therefore . . . "

Hugo opened the black box. Inside I saw something that looked like colored macaroni attached to a board. There were also some little black buttons, tiny batteries, and a square that looked like licorice.

"This box," Hugo said, "only responds to a certain series of rings. I built it from scratch. It's an integrated circuit, but I just call it a memory box. Now, when you want to feed your goldfish, you call home, let the phone ring

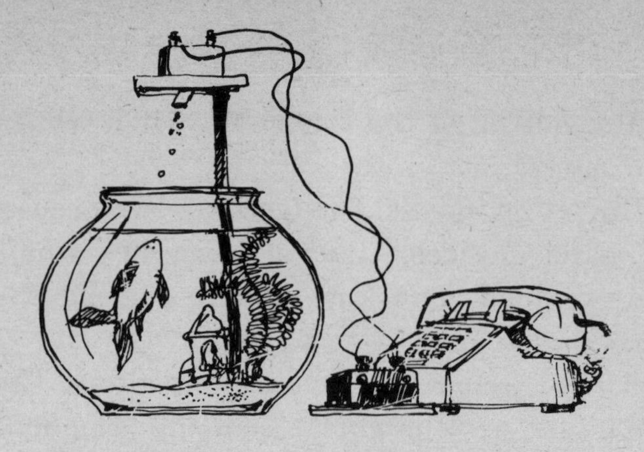

three times and hang up. You wait thirty seconds and call again. This time you let it ring twice."

Hugo showed us. All of a sudden a tiny bit of food dropped out of the bottom of a metal tube that was hanging above the goldfish bowl.

"It works!" I said. "Amazing!"

"We just get a neighbor to feed our goldfish when we're away," Rachel said. She went back to her solar house.

"Hugo," I whispered, "do you think the person who stole your plans will try to copy this exhibit?"

Hugo shook his head. "It's impossible. That memory box took me weeks to build."

Will said, "I don't like it. Something is going on and that Lester is the only kid at Monrose with any real brains."

"Lester only uses his brains to cheat," I said.

"Everyone at Monrose cheats. That is their specialty."

Will took me aside. "Toria, we have to be ready for anything. We have to have very tight security. Now Chuck and I have a plan—"

"Where *is* Chuck?" I asked.

"He'll be right back." Will pulled a piece of paper out of his pocket. It was a diagram of the gym. "Listen," Will said. "I will be here—at this table. Chuck will stand in front of Hugo's table the whole time to make sure no one 'accidentally' bumps into it . . . "

"What about me?" I asked. "What do I do?"

"Melt into the crowd," Will said. "You know, snoop around, look for troublemakers, report anything that looks suspicious."

"I get it! Just like the Secret Service." I said. "Wow! All we need are some walkie-talkies!"

"Chuck went up to the science room to ask Mr. Molinaro if he could get us some," Will said.

I was impressed. Then I remembered my solar house. "Just a minute," I said to Will.

I dumped my solar house on Rachel's table.

"Hey!" Rachel said. "I already have one."

"Well, now you have two," I said, and I ran back to Will.

"We're forgetting one thing," I said to Will. "We need a name—you know, a code name for the operation."

Will grinned. He looked at his watch. "It is now eight-fifteen. The Monrose Monsters are due to arrive in forty-five minutes. At exactly nine o'clock OPERATION GOLDFISH begins!"

8:30 A. M.

Chuck just got back from the science room.

"I couldn't get the walkie-talkies," he said. He seemed very discouraged.

"Did you tell Mr. Molinaro that Hugo's plans were stolen?" Will asked.

Chuck nodded. "But I'm afraid Mr. Molinaro is not taking us seriously. He said we could use some orange juice cans for walkie-talkies."

Will stared at Chuck. "What? In this crowd?"

"Wait a minute." Hugo tapped Will on the shoulder. "My brother has a set of walkie-talkies. I'll go get them."

8:50 A. M.

The Monrose Monsters have just arrived—ten minutes early. Hugo's not back yet, but OPERATION GOLDFISH has begun.

"Should I start melting into the crowd?" I asked Will.

Red Jamieson walked in carrying a goldfish bowl. Gretchen Messer was right behind him with a telephone.

"I knew it!" Will said. "All they need is that memory box. I'm sure there's going to be an attempt to get it away from Hugo."

"In the middle of a Science Fair?" I asked. "In broad daylight?"

"Look Toria," Will said, "as soon as Hugo gets back here, you find Lester and put a tail on him. He's the one I want you to follow. He's the brains behind this."

Just then we saw Hugo running toward us. He had a funny look on his face.

"What's the matter?" Will asked him.

Hugo was out of breath. "One . . . one of the walkie-talkies disappeared. It was in my pocket when I came in, but now it's gone! I've been looking all over the hallway, but it's very crowded out there."

"I'll go look," I said.

"Hold on, Toria." Will turned to Hugo. "Where's the other walkie-talkie?"

"Here." Hugo pulled a walkie-talkie out of his jacket pocket. "The missing one was in the other pocket," he said. "My brother will kill me if anything happens to it. He made these himself. I didn't even ask if I could borrow them. He wasn't home."

"*Hello, Hugo,*" a voice said. It was a high, squeaky voice.

We all looked around to see who was talking.

"*Hugo, we seem to have something that belongs to you.*" The voice was coming from the walkie-talkie!

Hugo was staring at the walkie-talkie in his hand.

"Answer them," Will whispered.

Hugo pushed a button on the walkie-talkie. "Who is this?" Hugo's voice was shaky.

"This is a nice walkie-talkie," the high voice said.

"Well, give it back, whoever-you-are," Hugo said. "It happens to belong to my brother. He made it himself."

"You have a smart family, Hugo," the voice said. *"Now I wouldn't mention this to anyone if I were you. In fact, if you move away from that table, you will never get this walkie-talkie back in one piece."*

I looked around the gym. The Monrose Monsters were quietly setting up exhibits. Red Jamieson was reading a comic book. The whole scene was creepy.

"Now I have a friend," the voice went on, *"who wishes to put this walkie-talkie into a bowl full of goldfish."*

"No!" Hugo shouted. "Don't do that! You'll ruin it. Tell me what you want!"

"All we want is that black box you built, the wires, and the metal tube. We brought our own goldfish food—"

"You're crazy," Hugo said. "I spent weeks working on this exhibit."

All at once we heard a click. Then there was silence.

"Wait a minute," Hugo yelled. "Please don't put it in a goldfish bowl. Listen . . . I'll do whatever you say. I've got to have the walkie-talkie back!"

There was some static on the walkie-talkie. Then that voice again.

"Listen carefully, Hugo. Put that equipment we want into a large manila envelope. Wait where you are until twelve o'clock."

"Where should I meet you?" Hugo sounded strangely calm.

"You won't meet us at all. At twelve o'clock you go out to the football field—alone. *If we see any of your little friends around that football field this afternoon, your brother will have a very wet walkie-talkie. Understand?"* The voice had become lower.

"I understand," Hugo said. "Go on."

"Under the bleachers—third row, dead center, you will see a small shovel. You are to bury the envelope right under that shovel. Then return to your table and stay there until the judging is over."

"When do I get the walkie-talkie back?" Hugo asked.

"At three o'clock you return to the same spot.

Your walkie-talkie will be in the hole. We'll even wrap it up for you. Got it?"

"Yes," Hugo said.

"*You will not be hearing from us again,*" the high voice said. There was a click.

We looked at each other.

"Hugo, you do just what they say," Will said. "Chuck, stay where you are. And Toria, you're coming with me."

"Where are we going, Will?" I asked.

"Up to the science room. We will be able to see the whole football field from there. They're not getting away with this. We are going to stake out that field!"

12:00 P. M.

Will and I are sitting in front of the windows of the science room watching the field through a pair of binoculars.

"Here comes Hugo," Will said.

I watched Hugo walk across the field. He was carrying the envelope containing the memory box. He disappeared under the bleachers. A few minutes later Hugo returned.

He was no longer carrying the envelope.

12:04 P. M.

A jogger just came out on the field and is running around the track.

"He runs a little funny," I said to Will, "but he looks pretty good in that sweatsuit."

The jogger stopped and did some stretching exercises.

"Not bad," Will said, "considering that Mr. Molinaro has never jogged in his life!"

"Did he think of putting that handkerchief around his head?" I asked.

"I guess so," Will said.

"Nice touch," I said. "Very authentic."

I looked Mr. Molinaro over carefully through the binoculars. He is part of our undercover operation, but he is not supposed to do anything until the walkie-talkie is safely buried.

"Oh, no!" I suddenly said.

"What's the matter?" Will asked.

"Do joggers ever wear heavy black lace-up shoes?"

Will grabbed the binoculars and looked.

He groaned. "Doesn't Mr. Molinaro know that the shoes are the most important thing?"

"We can't do anything now," I said. "It's too late. Let's just hope they don't notice."

12:30 P. M.

No one has appeared yet. The judging doesn't take place until two o'clock and Mr. Molinaro already looks quite tired. He hasn't been jogging for the last fifteen minutes. He has been sitting on the grass panting.

"Toria," Will whispered. "Look!"

Lester was heading across the field toward the bleachers. He was carrying the walkie-talkie; I could see it clearly through the binoculars. In his other hand he had a plastic bag full of water.

Mr. Molinaro jumped to his feet and began running around the track again.

Lester stopped for a moment and watched Mr. Molinaro. Then he went on.

"He doesn't suspect anything," I whispered. "Look, he just dumped the bag of water and he's putting the walkie-talkie into another plastic bag."

Will and I watched as Lester disappeared under the bleachers.

12:40 P. M.

Lester hasn't come out yet.

"What's taking him so long?" I asked. "He just had to switch two things."

"Keep your eyes on that field, Toria," Will said. "Make sure no one goes near those bleachers."

Just then Lester appeared. He had his hands in his pockets. He strolled away from the bleachers. Mr. Molinaro ran over and stopped him.

"Hey!" Will jumped to his feet. "What's going on? *Lester doesn't have the envelope!*"

I looked. Lester was letting Mr. Molinaro search him.

"He doesn't seem to have the walkie-talkie either!" I said.

"Let's go." Will grabbed his jacket. "Something went wrong. Lester must have caught on to our stakeout!"

1:30 P. M.

The envelope was still in the hole where Hugo buried it. The memory box was in the envelope safe and sound.

But the walkie-talkie was nowhere to be seen!

For the last hour we have been searching all over. We examined every bit of ground under the bleachers. No ground has been disturbed except for the hole with the envelope in it. Will doesn't want the envelope moved.

"We shouldn't disturb anything," he said.

We searched every corner of the bleachers.

Lester watched us. "Want some help?" he just asked me. He has an ugly smile.

"Could he have thrown it someplace?" Mr. Molinaro asked.

"We should look in the surrounding area," Will said. "Just in case."

Will and I walked in circles around the bleachers checking every inch of ground. I began to get tired.

"Look, Will," I finally said. "Maybe Lester is innocent. Maybe we dreamed this whole thing. That walkie-talkie disappeared into thin air."

"Impossible," Will snapped. He was getting tired too. "Look, Lester knew he was being watched, so he left the memory box where it was. Then, somehow, he got rid of that walkie-talkie. We just haven't figured out how . . . "

Suddenly Will stopped walking. "I read this book once . . . " he said slowly. "It was about the criminal mind. You know, it is very hard to think the way criminals think—even if you are just as smart."

"Why is that, Will?" I wasn't really interested.

"Because criminals are dishonest," Will said. "They think dishonestly."

"No kidding," I said. I couldn't believe Will was talking this way!

"Match his mind." Will looked over at Lester. "I have to think the way he thinks."

Will went over to Lester, who was sitting on the bleachers. I watched Will. For the next few minutes Will imitated everything Lester did. When Lester crossed his legs, Will crossed his legs. Will even imitated the expression on Lester's face.

"Cut it out," Lester said with a sniff.

"Cut it out," Will said with a sniff.

Suddenly Lester stood up and went to Mr. Molinaro, who was checking the bleacher seats for the third time.

"Can I go now?" Lester asked him.

Mr. Molinaro looked down at Will.

"Well, I guess we'll have to let him go soon. We just don't have any evidence," he said.

Lester smiled. Lester has a lot of teeth. I saw Will smile—just the way Lester smiled. It was horrible. Will was beginning to look like Lester!

Will suddenly jumped up. "I've got it!" he shouted. "I matched his mind. I got inside his head. I am thinking just like him. And I know where he hid that walkie-talkie!"

Will did know! Try to guess where Lester hid the walkie-talkie before you turn this page. . . .

*T*A*C*K Secret Service: Operation Goldfish*

Will's Solution:

Lester had buried the walkie-talkie in a hole *under* the envelope with the memory box in it. There was a hole *under* the hole! No one had thought of digging deeper in the same place—at least not until Will "matched" Lester's mind.

When Lester noticed Mr. Molinaro running around the track, he got suspicious. He decided to drop his plan and get rid of the walkie-talkie. He didn't want to get into trouble.

Now Lester is in plenty of trouble: He will never be allowed at another Science Fair. On top of that, his old buddy Red Jamieson says he's going to punch Lester's nose through his face for "messing up."

The judging took place at two o'clock and Hugo won first prize for his exhibit.

To everyone's surprise Will's slime got an honorable mention. My solar house didn't get a thing.

The Locked House Mystery

SANDY HARBOR, TUESDAY, DECEMBER 26—

It snowed all Christmas Day and it is still snowing. Everything looks beautiful.

Will and his younger brother Cyrus are going to stay at our house for a few days. Their parents have gone away on a skiing trip. Their parents go skiing every year, but usually Will and Cyrus stay with their Aunt Christobel.

Aunt Christobel is not very good with children. Last year she made Will and Cyrus do exercises three times a day to improve their posture. She corrected their grammar so much, "I stopped talking," Cyrus told us later. "But we still had to have good manners all the time. Millions of manners—manners I never even heard of."

Will and Cyrus were delighted to be invited to our house this year.

They arrived here this morning right before lunch. My little sister Holly ran to meet them at the front door. She was trying to be "The Perfect Hostess".

"Give me that," she said grabbing Cyrus's overnight bag. "Toria," she whispered. "You are supposed to carry Will's suitcase. He is your guest."

We all followed Holly up the stairs. When we came to Holly's room, she dropped the bag on the floor. "This is where you will sleep," she said. "That bed is yours, Cyrus. Don't you love the pillowcase? It's mine, but I am going to let you use it."

"Wow!" Cyrus grinned. "It has a Blurpy on it." (Blurpy is a cartoon character that seems to appeal to younger children.) "It's very nice," Cyrus said.

"*Very* nice," Holly agreed, "and very nice of me to let you use it. Oh look! Stuffy likes you, Cyrus."

Stuffy is our orange and white cat. She was rubbing up against Cyrus and purring loudly. Cyrus bent down to pet Stuffy.

"No, Cyrus!" Will grabbed Cyrus and pulled him back. "Don't touch that cat!"

Holly and I stared at Will.

"Cyrus is allergic to cats," Will explained. "But it's all right. He brought his allergy pills with him. They really work."

"I love cats," Cyrus said sadly.

After lunch Will and I went outside and had a snow fight. We stayed out most of the afternoon.

When we came inside, we found a huge fire

going in the living room fireplace. Holly and Cyrus were sitting in front of the fire playing Monopoly. My mother brought us all hot chocolate with marshmallows. It was very cozy.

Will and I sat on the window seat looking out at the snow. We watched it get dark. We didn't say anything. That's what's nice about having a friend like Will. We don't have to talk all the time.

It was very quiet except for the crackling of the fire. Then I heard another sound—a strange sniffling-snorting sound. The sniffling sound got worse. I looked at Cyrus. He was rubbing his eyes. Stuffy was curled up on his lap. I went and picked Stuffy off Cyrus's lap.

"Hey, Toria, don't do that!" Holly yelled at me. "Stuffy was comfortable."

Then I saw Cyrus's face. I got a shock. Tears were dripping from his eyes. His nose was swollen and his whole face was very red.

"Will! Help!" I called. "Look at Cyrus!"

Will came over. "Cyrus," he said. "You'd better take an allergy pill right now!"

"I'm all right," Cyrus muttered.

"I'll go get your pills," Will said. "Where are they?" Will seemed a little scared.

Cyrus looked down and sniffled. He didn't say anything.

Holly was drumming her fingers on the Monopoly board. "Hurry up! Hurry up! C'mon Cyrus, it's your turn to go."

"Holly," I said, "it's more than a little cruel of you to think of a game at a time like this. I'm getting Mom."

"No!" Cyrus said. He rubbed his eyes and rolled the dice. "Please don't tell."

"Tell what?" Will asked him. "Where are your pills?"

"Um, Will." Cyrus sniffed. "Do you happen to remember that big note on the kitchen table . . ."

"You mean the note that said, 'CYRUS, DO NOT FORGET PILLS'?" Will was watching Cyrus.

"Well, it didn't exactly say that," Cyrus said. "It said, 'CYRUS, DO NOT FORGET PILLS AND HOUSE KEY.'"

"Cyrus." Will spoke very slowly. "By any chance, are your pills locked in our house along with our house key?"

"In a way," Cyrus mumbled.

"In a way?" Will asked. "What do you mean by that?"

"Oh Will, please don't tell. I'm all right. Really I am! I don't need the pills. *Please don't make me go to Aunt Christobel's.*"

Tears were pouring down Cyrus's cheeks, but it was hard to tell if he was crying or not.

"He looks terrible," I said.

Holly looked up and said thoughtfully, "You do look terrible." Then she said, "And you owe me two hundred dollars for landing on my railroad."

Everyone was miserable at the dinner table. My mother didn't know what to do about Cyrus. Cyrus sat at the table wheezing and sniffling and saying he was all right. But everyone could see he was having trouble breathing.

Mom tried to call his parents, but she couldn't reach them. Then she tried Cyrus's doctor, Dr. Winkler.

"I left a message with his answering service," she said. "I hope he calls soon."

Stuffy was locked up in the den. "Not that it will do any good," Mom said. "There are cat hairs all over this house." We sat in silence listening to Stuffy howling and scratching at the door.

"It's not fair to Stuffy," Holly kept saying. "Stuffy lives here. She can't help it if Cyrus forgot his dumb old pills."

"Holly!" my mother said.

"Cyrus is the one who should be locked up," Holly said.

"I don't mind," Cyrus mumbled.

Just then the telephone rang. My mother ran to answer it. We all tried to hear what she was saying.

". . . too late to get a prescription filled. Yes, Dr. Winkler, I guess a cat-free house would be best. Yes, I'll call Christobel Roberts right away. Thank you."

"Wait!" Will shouted. "Don't call her yet, Mrs. Gardner. I just remembered. I'm sure there's an extra key to the house. My parents hide it on the ledge above the back door—"

"Let's go, Will," I said. I ran to get my boots and jacket.

"Hold it, children," my mother said. "It's already eight o'clock. If you are not back here with those pills before nine, I will have to call Christobel. She goes to bed early."

"But, Mom," I pleaded. "It takes fifteen minutes to get to Will's house and fifteen minutes to get back."

"Well, we can't drive you there. The car is snowed in," my mother said. "At nine o'clock I am calling Christobel—whether you're back or not. Cyrus cannot sleep in this house unless he has those pills."

"Don't worry," I whispered to Cyrus. "We'll do our best."

"Thanks, Toria." Cyrus sniffled.

The snow had stopped falling. The snow drifts made blue shadows in the moonlight. Our voices echoed as we made our way through the snow. It was exciting to be out on a mission at night.

When we finally got to Will's house, we trudged through the snow to the back door.

"Wait a minute," Will said. "There's a ladder in the garage. We're going to need it. I'll get it."

I stood on the back stoop and looked up at the ledge. It was covered with snow.

"I can't get the garage door open!" Will called. "It's locked!"

"Oh no!" I looked up at the ledge. I tried to jump up.

"I know!" Will said. "There's an old broom next to this garbage can. It's probably buried under the snow . . . "

Will dug very fast and came up with the broom. Very carefully, he began to sweep the snow off the ledge. Then he stopped.

"I'm afraid I might knock the key off," he said. "If we lose it in the snow, we'll never find it in the dark. We really need a ladder."

"Borrow a ladder from the Foxes," I said. The Foxes are Will's neighbors. They are his only neighbors. Will's house is on a pretty lonely road.

"They're away on vacation," Will said. "And

if we go back to your house to get one, we'll lose too much time."

"We've got to climb on something," I said.

Will and I looked at each other. We both got the idea at the same time.

Will bent down. I climbed onto his shoulders. He held me steady by my boots and began walking toward the ledge. I sat on his shoulders and stretched my arms up as far as they could go.

"I can't even reach the ledge," I wailed. "Hey, maybe, if I *stand* on your shoulders . . . " I put one foot up. Then I changed my mind. "Nope," I said. "Too dangerous. Oh, Will, can't you jump?"

"No, Toria," Will said. "I cannot jump. I cannot see either. You know, it is quite difficult to see with icy wet mittens over your eyes."

"Sorry, Will." I moved my hands.

"I've got it!" Will said. "We're doing this all wrong."

"You're telling me," I said.

"Let *me* sit on *your* shoulders!" Will said.

"But I'm smaller," I said. "The smaller person is *supposed* to sit on top. Everyone does it that way. Besides, what good would it do? It's the same height when you add us together."

"But there's an important difference," Will said. "My arms are longer."

"I don't see . . . oh yeah," I said. I was getting a little cross at Will. He seemed to have a lot of answers, but we weren't getting anyplace. And we were running out of time!

Will and I changed places. Will climbed on my shoulders. I kept saying things like "Hurry up!" and *"This better work!"*

"Don't say that," Will said. "It doesn't help."

Will is taller than I am, but he doesn't weigh much more. Even so, I had trouble keeping my balance. The snow on the stoop was beginning to get slippery.

"No, Toria!" Will called down to me. "Step forward! The other way! Not backward! Toward the ledge! Forward! Forward!"

"I'm trying to," I muttered.

But it was much too slippery. Before I knew it, I had stepped right off the back stoop. Will and I were lying in a snowdrift.

Will was laughing. "You . . . you . . . kept going the wrong way!" he said.

"Well, I couldn't help it," I said.

I waited for Will to stop laughing. But he was rolling around and around in the snow. "Every time I said, 'Forward,' you took another step backward," and he laughed some more.

I began to feel quite angry.

"All right, Will," I said. "So I made a little mistake. But this is not a good time to laugh in the snow. Think of poor Cyrus and how he is suffering. Think of five days with dear Aunt Christobel . . ."

But Will wouldn't stop.

"Will," I said. "Be serious! Get up right this minute. We've got to figure this out. Laughing doesn't help!"

Will flopped over and looked at me. "But it does help, Toria," he said. "Laughing *does* help." He sighed happily. "Don't you see? We won't have any trouble reaching that key. The answer has been here all along. We just didn't see it."

Will's plan was simple. And it worked! Can you guess how we got that key off the ledge before you turn the page?

The Locked House Mystery

Will's Solution:

There was snow all around us. Quickly we piled up snow on the back stoop. We packed it until it got higher and higher. Then Will climbed on the mound of snow and got the key.

You should have seen Cyrus's face when we got back with his pills.

"Oh boy!" he shouted. "I can stay!"

"I *told* you they'd get them," Holly said.

The Pirates of Sandy Harbor

SANDY HARBOR, FRIDAY, JANUARY 26—

"How does this sound?" I asked Chuck. "*Three hundred years ago Sandy Harbor was crawling with pirates. A local boatbuilder named Simon Hawk chased the pirates away. Later he became the founder of the Independent Village of Sandy Harbor.*

"Sounds great," Chuck said.

Chuck and I were sitting in the town library. This year is the 300th birthday of Sandy Harbor. Everyone in our class has to do a report on local history.

"But Chuck," I said, "that's all I could find on Simon Hawk. There's one dusty old pamphlet in this whole library and our reports are due in two weeks! This won't fill up a whole page. It won't even fill up half a page."

"Write big," Chuck said. I gave him a dirty

look. "Sorry, Toria," he said. "I was only kidding. Look, why don't you just add some stuff about pirates in general? You know—about some of the things they did."

"Big deal," I said coldly. "What did pirates do that was so interesting besides killing, torturing, stealing, blowing up ships, and chopping off people's heads?"

Chuck laughed. "Well, maybe you could make it *sound* interesting."

I watched Chuck work. Chuck has collected a lot of material on his subject. He picked the Great Sandy Harbor Flood. That flood happened only thirty years ago, so there are plenty of newspaper articles and pictures. He also talked to people in town who remember the flood and told him plenty of stories about it.

"What's Will doing his report on?" I asked Chuck.

"Pickles," Chuck said. "He's very excited about it. He says he's working on a recipe that's two hundred years old. He got it from his grandmother. It was never written down so he's testing it."

"Historical pickles?" I asked.

Chuck nodded and turned a page in the old

newspaper he was reading. "Wow! Toria, look at this." He showed me a photograph of our main street. It was completely flooded. A small motorboat was tied to a tree in front of our Post Office.

"Amazing!" Chuck said. "I can't believe it! But what am I going to do? I have so much great stuff. How will I ever fit it all into one report?"

"Write small," I said, and I left the library.

After dinner tonight I just sat at my desk staring at a blank piece of paper.

"Anything the matter, Toria?" My father was standing at the door.

I told him about Simon Hawk. "There's nothing on him," I said.

"Why don't you speak to Mr. Hawk?" my father said.

"Very funny, Popsy. Ha. Ha." I was in a terrible mood. "Simon Hawk's only been dead a few hundred years."

"Not Simon," Popsy said. "William Hawk—the director of the Sandy Harbor Historical Society. It's in that little white house behind the library. He's very nice, and I believe his family is related to old Simon."

SANDY HARBOR, SATURDAY, JANUARY 27—

I was a little nervous when I walked into the Historical Society.

"Mr. William Hawk, please," I said to a lady behind a desk in the front hall.

"Mr. Hawk is in with Mr. Parks right now," the lady said.

"You mean Harrison Parks, the editor of the *Sandy Harbor Herald*?" I asked.

"Yes," the lady sighed. "This place has been a madhouse all morning—after that article in this morning's *Herald*."

"What article?" I asked.

She handed me a copy of the newspaper. "Page four," she said. "Why don't you just take it to the bench outside Mr. Hawk's office." She pointed down the hall.

I sat down and turned to page four.

SEA CHEST FOUND

An old sea chest believed to have belonged to Simon Hawk, the founder of Sandy Harbor, turned up in a local antique shop last week. The chest and its contents were immediately turned over to the Sandy Harbor Historical Society.

There are reports that a note written by Mr. Hawk himself was found in the chest.

Mr. William E. Hawk, director of the society, confirmed that the sea chest belonged to Simon Hawk. He said a monogram on the side is identical to those found on his boat models. However, Mr. Hawk denies there is proof that the note was written by Simon Hawk.

The contents of the note have not been released to the public at this time.

I read it over again. I could hear voices inside Mr. Hawk's office, but I couldn't hear what they were saying.

Then I noticed a painting hanging on the wall across from the bench. It was full of old sailing ships. I love sailboats. I stood up and went to look at it. It was an old painting of Sandy Harbor! I could recognize Corkhill Island, which is right across the bay from our

boat docks. There was a plaque at the bottom. I read it:

SIMON HAWK SETS SAIL ON HIS PIRATE CHASER,
THE PEMAQUID, IN PURSUIT OF CAPTAIN HORATIO SLY.
CAPTAIN SLY WAS ATTACKING *STAR OF INDIA,*
A CARGO SHIP THAT HAD GONE AGROUND
ON THE ROCKY SHOALS OFF CORKHILL ISLAND.

*(Donated by the estate
of Merriwether Stephens)*

I looked at that painting for a long time. Then I went and sat down on the bench.

Fifteen minutes went by. I was still waiting. Then an hour. I began to feel sleepy. I stared at the painting.

Suddenly I heard loud voices. The door to Mr. Hawk's office was open. Mr. Parks was on his way out.

"Look, Bill," Mr. Parks was saying, "you know as well as I do what that note proves. It proves that Simon Hawk was working with Horatio Sly. He was working with the pirates!"

"It's too early to say." Mr. Hawk had a quiet, gentle voice. "We need time to study this."

"Well, the way it stands it certainly looks

bad for old Simon Hawk. It looks as if he actually *planned* the attack on the *Star of India*!" Mr. Parks sounded very excited. "Now I know you're a fine historian," he said, "but I'm a newspaperman. This is a big story. I'm publishing that note the way it stands!"

"I can't stop you," Mr. Hawk said, "but I feel you are making a terrible mistake. That note was in pieces and the paper is three hundred years old! We can't just fit it together like a jigsaw puzzle."

Mr. Hawk closed the door to his office.

Harrison Parks rushed past me rubbing his hands together.

I jumped to my feet and knocked on Mr. Hawk's office door.

"Yes?" Mr. Hawk opened it. He was tall and very thin. He had lots of soft white hair that fell over his forehead.

I started talking very fast. "Hello, my name is Toria Gardner. I'm doing my school report on Simon Hawk—it's due in two weeks."

I suddenly noticed that Mr. Hawk was staring at me blankly. "Two weeks sounds just fine," he said. "I'll be happy to see you in two weeks," and he closed the door.

For a moment I just stood there.

Now what was I going to write?

All at once I realized I didn't care about my article anymore. I cared about Simon Hawk!

By tomorrow morning the whole town would think Simon Hawk was working with the pirates, that he was just another pirate. *But what if he were innocent?*

I ran as fast as I could to the library. I knew I would find Chuck there.

He stared at my face. "Toria!" he said. "What's wrong?"

"We've got to get Will," I panted.

"Right," Chuck said. "Let's go!" He didn't ask any questions.

Will was in his kitchen. He was wearing a white apron. He was pouring sugar into a big glass jar full of cucumbers and a cloudy liquid. An iron pot was boiling on the stove. Will turned to look at us as we marched in.

"Will," I said grimly. "Drop the pickles. It looks like we have a job for T*A*C*K."

I told Will and Chuck the whole story.

"But, Toria," Will said. "That kind of thing happened a lot. Pirate chasers very often turned into pirates themselves."

"Simon Hawk is innocent until proven guilty," I said.

"Of course," Will said. He took off his apron. "Just tell us where to start."

I thought for a minute. "There's a painting I want you to look at," I said.

Will, Chuck, and I stood in front of the big, dark painting in the Historical Society.

"But Toria," Chuck said. "I don't see anything wrong with that painting."

"Something keeps bothering me," I said. "There's something the matter with it."

Will and Chuck stared at the painting.

"Wait a minute!" I shouted. "I know what it is. The *Star of India* couldn't go aground over there. It's too deep. The rocky shoals are on the other side of Corkhill Island. The painting is crazy. It's all wrong!"

A man was standing behind us, but I was too excited to pay much attention.

"Maybe the bottom of the harbor changed," Will suggested, "in three hundred years."

"Well," I said, "sand can shift around, but rocks don't change much—do they?" I asked the man who was now beside me looking up at the painting.

"No, they don't," he said.

I suddenly realized I was talking to William E. Hawk!

"Oops," I said and I covered my mouth.

"Young lady, do you know that hundreds of people have looked at that painting"—Mr. Hawk seemed pleased—"but you're the only one I've ever come across who noticed that mistake."

"You already knew?" I asked. He nodded.

"Then," I said, "if the painting is wrong, is the whole story wrong—about Simon Hawk chasing the pirates?"

"No," he said. "The artist just wanted an exciting painting. If the *Star of India* were aground in the right place, you wouldn't be able to see it in the painting."

"Wow!" I said. "You can't believe anything, can you?"

Mr. Hawk laughed. "Aren't you the young lady doing some research on Simon Hawk?" he asked me.

"It's due in two weeks," Chuck volunteered.

"That doesn't matter," I said. "Mr. Hawk, I

heard you talking to Mr. Parks. I am not going to write a word about Simon Hawk until we know the truth—no matter how long it takes."

"But Toria," Chuck whispered. "You'll fail the assignment."

"I don't care," I said. "It's much more important to know whether Simon Hawk was working with the pirates or not. It's not fair to accuse someone who isn't even around to defend himself—not without definite proof!"

Mr. Hawk was looking at me. He seemed to be making up his mind about something.

Suddenly he clapped his hands. "Come with me," he said. "You too," he said to Will and Chuck. "I want you to take a look at something."

We followed him into his office. On his desk were two sheets of glass stuck together. In between were pieces of paper.

"Remember," Mr. Hawk said, "no one has ever seen Simon Hawk's handwriting."

"THE NOTE!" I gasped. I stood beside Mr. Hawk and read the pieced-together note. It certainly looked bad for Simon Hawk!

"Wasn't this note found in Simon Hawk's sea chest?" I asked Mr. Hawk.

"Yes," Mr. Hawk said.

"Why would Simon Hawk keep his own note?" I asked.

"Good point," Mr. Hawk said. "But I'm afraid it didn't impress Harrison Parks. But that's not the only thing that bothers me. I have a funny feeling about this note. Something's wrong—you know. I feel the same way you felt about that painting."

Chuck and I were standing next to Mr. Hawk. Will was on the other side of his desk.

"Will," I whispered, "come here. You can see it better from here. Will . . . "

Will didn't move. He just stood there staring at the pieces of paper in the glass. I felt he was being a bit rude.

"Will," I said again, "come over here and look at it the right way!"

Will hesitated. Then he came around to join us.

"Simon Hawk didn't sign that note," Will said. "He found it. That's how he knew when Sly was going to attack!"

Suddenly Will seemed embarrassed. "At least, that's what I think."

"Well, well, well," Mr. Hawk said. "Let's hear your theory."

Simon Hawk didn't sign that note. Will's theory was correct. Can you figure it out?

The Pirates of Sandy Harbor

Will's Solution:

The note was signed by someone with the initial *H*. It was not signed by Simon Hawk. The pieces had been put together wrong. *SIMON* was actually *NOW IS* upside down.

This is how the note really fit together:

Before we knew it, William Hawk was on the phone to Harrison Parks. "Stop the presses, Harrison," he said. "I don't want you to make a fool of yourself. There are some young people I'd like you to meet. Can you drop by?"

The Dance of the Trees

SANDY HARBOR, SATURDAY, FEBRUARY 23—

Every Saturday I have to pick up my little sister Holly at Madame Lyubova's Ballet School. Usually I try to get there early. I like to peek through the curtain at the little kids dancing around on the wooden floor.

This morning I was a little late. Holly was in the changing room buttoning her winter jacket over her pink leotard and tights.

"Who got the part?" I asked Holly.

Today was the day their class had tryouts for the lead in a ballet called *The Dance of the Trees*. Madame Lyubova's Ballet School will be having its spring recital next month. Each class will perform a different number. All week Holly has been telling everyone that she is going to be the Tree Fairy in *The Dance of the Trees*.

Holly was stuffing her pink ballet shoes into her ballet bag. She looked furious. I figured she didn't get the part.

"Hi, Toria!"

I turned around. Two little girls in pink leotards were waving shyly at me.

I went over to talk to them. "Hi, Gussie. Hi, Samantha. Which is which? I know. You're Gussie and you're Samantha."

The two girls shook their heads. I felt bad. Gussie and Samantha are identical twins. Everyone always gets them mixed up.

I took them aside and whispered, "Who got the part? Who's going to be Tree Fairy?"

Gussie and Samantha looked at each other.

"Alexandra got it," Samantha said.

"It isn't fair," said Gussie. "She only got it because she is better than everyone else."

"Yeah," Samantha grumbled. "Just because she's better. That's the only reason."

I tried not to smile. "So everyone else is a tree?" I asked.

They nodded.

"But aren't you excited?" I asked. "The performance will be in a real theater. Everyone in Sandy Harbor will be there . . . "

Then I saw Holly heading out the door.

" 'Bye, Holly," Gussie and Samantha called.

But Holly didn't answer. She didn't even turn around.

I caught up to Holly on the sidewalk. Holly was walking very fast. She was staring straight ahead. She looked as if she were going to explode.

When we got to our front door, Holly suddenly dropped her ballet bag and collapsed on the stoop. She buried her head in her lap and began to cry.

"Just another tree," she sobbed. "I'm just another tree!"

"Oh, Holly . . . " I didn't know what else to say.

SATURDAY, MARCH 8—

When I arrived at the ballet school this morning, Holly ran to meet me.

"Oh, Toria! Wait till you see! Wait till you see what we're going to wear. We have this brown satin trunk around us all the way to the floor and our arms and heads are all covered with leaves—and, oh, Toria! Guess what! We will even have brown satin ballet shoes to match. It's beautiful! Much nicer than Alexandra's costume. She just wears this dumb fluffy white dress."

To my surprise Chuck and Will were standing in the studio talking to Madame Lyubova. I waited for them to finish.

They both looked pleased when they came out.

"Oh, boy!" Will said. "Madame Lyubova is going to let us do it! She likes the idea!"

"Do what?" I asked.

"Make mist," Chuck said. "You see, my

father is building the sets for this recital and we were helping him paint some forest scenery—"

"For *The Dance of the Trees*?" I asked.

"Yup," Chuck said. "And I got an idea. You see, you just put dry ice in buckets. Then you pour water over the ice and it makes white mist. Lots and lots of it. Then you take a fan and blow it around the stage, but it stays near the ground so you can still see the dancers."

"We've already tried it out," Will told me. "It really looks professional."

I was very excited. "I can't wait to see it," I said.

SATURDAY, MARCH 15—

The recital will be held next Saturday at the Sandy Harbor Theater. There will be dress rehearsals in the theater all this week. Madame Lyubova said I could watch.

This afternoon was the first dress rehearsal. When the curtain rose on *The Dance of the Trees,* I gasped. The forest looked so real and the mist was just wonderful. There was only one trouble. The little trees forgot to dance.

They just stood there staring down at the mist swirling around their feet.

"Once again," Madame Lyubova called. "From the beginning!"

The next time the music started, the mist swirled around and the little trees began to sway in the breeze. It seemed just perfect until two little trees came running in late. I started to giggle and had to go out into the lobby for a few minutes.

MONDAY, MARCH 17—

Alexandra is very good. She is a beautiful Tree Fairy. She seems to do everything right, but Madame Lyubova corrects her all the time. Alexandra listens carefully and then tries again. She is very patient. But Holly says it's much harder to be a tree. "*We* have to do everything exactly together," she told me.

TUESDAY, MARCH 18—

Every day I get more and more excited about the recital on Saturday. Today the older students rehearsed their number first. It is a modern ballet about cowboys.

Madame Lyubova was sitting right in front of me in the theater. She kept looking at her watch.

Then her older students rehearsed the cowboy ballet again . . . and again. . . .

Chuck and Will came out from backstage and sat down next to me in the auditorium.

"What's going on?" I asked. "What happened to *The Dance of the Trees*?"

"Alexandra isn't here yet," Will whispered. He took out his math book and began doing his homework.

Just then Madame Lyubova's assistant, a tall, thin dancer named Sonja, came running down the aisle.

"Alexandra is sick," she called to Madame Lyubova. "Her mother just called. Chicken pox. She can't dance!"

Madame Lyubova stared at Sonja. "Oh, no!" she said. "But it can't be!"

"Can we put off the recital?" Sonja asked.

"Impossible," Madame Lyubova said. "The theater is booked for this Saturday night. It was the only date we could get. And every single ticket is sold." She leaned on the seat in front of her and dropped her head on her arms. She just sat there for a few minutes.

Then she raised her head. "Sonja," she said, "call out the trees. I will have to tell them this terrible news."

A minute later we watched the twelve little trees file out into the auditorium. They knew something was wrong. They seemed so tired and sad. It was almost as if they had wilted!

The little trees sat down quietly in the front row and looked up at Madame Lyubova.

"Children," she began. "I don't know how to tell you this . . . " Madame Lyubova had tears in her eyes. The little trees looked at each other. "My darling little trees . . . "

When they found out that Alexandra had the chicken pox—that she couldn't dance—some of the trees moaned.

"Couldn't someone else learn the part?" one little girl asked.

"Not me!" Holly called out. "No one's going to make me be the Tree Fairy."

Madame Lyubova smiled at Holly. She shook her head sadly. "There are only four days. Four days is not enough time for someone else to learn the part."

"I know what!" another tree said. "Sonja could do it. She could be Tree Fairy. She made up the whole dance so she knows it even better than Alexandra." Everyone looked at Sonja.

Madame Lyubova's assistant shook her head. "I'm too big," Sonja said. "The Tree Fairy can't be bigger than all the trees. It would spoil everything."

A few little trees giggled, but the leading tree—a hard-working little girl named Nicole—burst into tears.

Will laid down his math book on the seat next to him.

"Excuse me, Madame Lyubova," Will said. All the little girls turned around to look at him. "How long would it take to teach another student the part?"

"Good question, Will," Madame Lyubova said. "It is true that children learn fast. Usually they can pick up steps much faster than adults—especially these little ones. But four days is not enough. We would need at least a week. You see, a dance is not just step, step, jump, jump, leap, leap. It is *how* it is done. No, no, we do it right or we do it not at all!"

"We don't need Alexandra," the Leading Tree sobbed. "We don't need the Tree Fairy."

"Yes, we do," Holly said. "She is the story. She is the most important person."

I felt very proud of Holly.

"I know!" Gussie suddenly jumped up. "You just put this pink toothpaste on Alexandra's spots and no one will know she has chicken pox—"

"That's right!" her twin sister yelled. "Gussie knows. She did that to her chicken pox."

Madame Lyubova put an arm around each twin and hugged them. "My dears," she said gently. "The doctor will not let her perform. I'm afraid we are going to have to cancel . . . "

"No!" Will shouted. He wrote some numbers in his math notebook. "I've got the answer!"

Will ran to the front of the auditorium and whispered something to Madame Lyubova and Sonja. Then I saw Sonja throw her arms around Will and kiss him.

"Well." Madame Lyubova was smiling. "It won't be perfect, but I believe it can be done. The performance will go on!"

Will's idea saved *The Dance of the Trees.* Can you try to figure it out before you turn the page?

The Dance of the Trees

Will's Solution:

The performance was tonight. When *The Dance of the Trees* was over, the audience clapped and clapped.

The Tree Fairy was wonderful—or, maybe I should say the Tree Fairy *were* wonderful.

You see, Gussie danced the role of Tree Fairy and then halfway through the ballet she disappeared behind the scenery and came out again.

Only this time the Tree Fairy was her twin sister Samantha. Only a few people knew. Each twin only had to learn half the dance, and four days was enough time to learn half.

After the recital, we all went out for ice cream. "I'm simply ravishing," Holly said. She was still wearing her costume.

"Don't you mean *ravenous*?" I asked.

But Holly couldn't keep her eyes open. Before we knew it, her leafy head was resting on the table right next to her chocolate marshmallow sundae.

"How adorable," the lady at the next table said.

A Slipper for Ripper

SANDY HARBOR, THURSDAY, APRIL 17—

Chuck has been very upset lately. His mother wants to get rid of his puppy, Duchess. Chuck has only had Duchess for a few months, but she is chewing up everything in the house. All the furniture has teeth marks on it, and last night she chewed up one of Chuck's father's fishing boots.

"One more toothmark in this house," Chuck's mother said, "and Duchess goes right back to the kennel."

Will and I had an emergency meeting this afternoon at the pet store. We wanted to buy Duchess a toy to chew so she wouldn't chew on other things. We brought Will's younger brother Cyrus along as our consultant. I showed Cyrus a whole rack full of dog toys. The sign over the rack read, TOYS THAT DOGS LOVE TO CHEW.

"Cyrus," I said. "If you were a dog, which toy would you like best?"

"If I were a dog . . . " Cyrus closed his eyes and thought for a few seconds. Then he opened his eyes. "What kind of dog?" he asked.

"A shaggy white puppy," Will said. "Just like Duchess."

"Oh," Cyrus said and he closed his eyes again. Then he opened his eyes and looked over the toys. He even sniffed a few of them.

"How about the rawhide bone with bells?" I asked. Cyrus shook his head.

"The rubber porcupine that squeaks?" Will asked him.

Cyrus didn't say anything.

"Oh, Cyrus, look at this little fire hydrant. Don't you think Duchess would enjoy that?" I asked.

"No," Cyrus said, "that is a toy for people. That is not a toy for dogs."

"Well, which one?" I asked. Cyrus was taking an awful long time deciding.

"None of them." Cyrus seemed very sure of himself. He went over to look at a display of cat toys.

Will shrugged. "Let's get Duchess the rawhide bone," he said.

"Wait a minute!" Cyrus called. He went to the man behind the counter.

"Mister," Cyrus said, "do you have any catnip for dogs?"

The man laughed. "No such thing," he told Cyrus.

"Oh." Cyrus looked puzzled. "How come?"

"C'mon, Cyrus," I called. "We're going to buy the bone. Thanks for helping anyway."

Chuck felt terrible when he found out that Will and I had spent our whole allowance on a toy for Duchess. "She already has a rawhide bone," Chuck said. "She has every toy in that pet store. She won't look at any of them."

THURSDAY, APRIL 24—

We have our fingers crossed. A whole week has gone by and Duchess has been very good. She hasn't chewed up anything. We are proud of her.

But Cyrus is disappointed. He has been working on a secret formula for dognip. "It won't be ready for another week," he told Chuck today.

"I don't think we'll need it, Cyrus." Chuck was very happy. "Duchess is growing up."

Cyrus looked so sad, Chuck said, "I'll tell you what. If Duchess is good for another whole week, you can give her your dognip as a reward."

That made Cyrus happy.

SATURDAY, MAY 3—

Today Cyrus is going to give Duchess her reward. Duchess hasn't chewed up anything for two whole weeks.

I met Will and Cyrus in front of Chuck's house. Cyrus was carrying a paper bag. He held it open for me. I looked inside.

"But that's just an old tennis ball," I said.

"Yes, but it's covered with dognip," Cyrus said.

"How nice," I said, and I rang Chuck's doorbell.

Chuck's mother opened the door.

"Chuck's been cleaning his room all day," she said. "He won't let me in. He wants to surprise me. Isn't that nice?"

I nodded and looked at Will.

"Something must be wrong," Will whispered to me as we went upstairs.

I knocked on Chuck's door.

"Who's there?" Chuck sounded frightened.

"It's us!" I called. "Cyrus wants to give Duchess her reward for being so good."

Chuck opened the door.

"Quick," Chuck whispered, "come in. I've got to put this stuffing back in my mattress before Mom finds out."

It seems that Duchess has been quietly chewing up Chuck's mattress from under the bed between the slats. There was gray, furry stuff all over the floor. "I noticed that stuff for the past two weeks, but I didn't know what it was." Chuck looked desperate.

"Can I give Duchess her reward now?" Cyrus asked.

We all turned and looked at Cyrus. Will sighed. "Look, Cyrus," he said, "why don't you just run out and give Duchess her present. We have a lot to do."

"Oh, boy!" Cyrus said and he left the room.

Will, Chuck, and I crawled under the bed

and began stuffing the furry bits into the holes in the mattress. When we finally finished, we put a piece of cardboard under the mattress to cover up the holes. Then we went downstairs and out into the backyard.

Cyrus ran to meet us. He was very excited.

"It's working! The dognip is working! She loves it!"

Duchess was lying in the grass chewing on the old tennis ball. Her tail was wagging. She seemed very happy with her new toy.

We were amazed. I said, "Cyrus, you're a genius. Please tell us how you make dognip."

Cyrus was so proud of himself, he told us. "But you have to promise not to tell," he said. "It doesn't cost a thing. You just wear the same socks for two weeks. Every night you put the tennis ball into the socks—"

"—so it absorbs the flavor?" Will asked.

Cyrus nodded. "As soon as Duchess smelled that dognip, she liked it. She liked it much better than the slipper."

"What slipper?" Chuck asked.

"The gold slipper," Cyrus said. "The one she was playing with."

"My mother has gold slippers." Chuck's voice was very faint.

"Don't worry," Cyrus said. "Duchess can't reach it now. I threw it over that hedge." He pointed.

I ran toward an opening in the hedge. "I'll go get it," I called.

"No, Toria!" Chuck screamed. "Ripper lives there!"

I froze. Ripper is a large Doberman pinscher. He is a vicious dog. Ever since he attacked the mailman, he has been kept on a chain. The chain is attached to a metal ring on a big oak tree right in the middle of the neighbor's backyard.

Chuck, Will, and I looked through the opening in the hedge. The gold slipper was lying right near the big black dog.

Then Ripper saw us. He leapt to his feet and ran toward us snarling. Luckily his chain doesn't reach the hedge. But Ripper was only a few feet away from us.

"I sure hope that chain doesn't break," I whispered. "Look at those fangs!"

"I've got to get that slipper," Chuck said and he crept slowly through the hedge. Ripper lunged at him, but the chain held him back. Chuck moved carefully around the edge of the neighbor's yard, keeping close to the hedge. Ripper followed him tugging at the end of his chain.

After a few minutes, Chuck gave up. He came back. "There's no way to get past that dog," he said.

"Call your neighbors," I suggested.

"They're not home," Chuck said. "They're hardly ever home. That's why they have a dog like Ripper. To scare people off."

"Look," Will said, "all we have to do is to figure out a way to get a slipper away from an animal who's not as smart as we are."

"He looks pretty smart to me," I said.

We sat down on the grass and thought.

"Well," Chuck said slowly. "We'll never find a stick that's long enough to reach . . ."

"Maybe we could lasso the slipper," I said.

"Good idea," Will said. "Do you have a long rope?" he asked Chuck.

"Well, there's that clothesline . . ." Chuck began.

Just then Chuck's mother came out.

"I'm going to the hairdresser," she told

Chuck. "I'll be back in an hour or so."

Chuck's mother suddenly noticed the tennis ball that Duchess was playing with.

"Where did you get this filthy old thing?" she asked. She grabbed it away from Duchess and threw it over the hedge. "It must belong to Ripper," she said.

We watched with our mouths open as she got into her car and drove down the driveway.

"Two whole weeks," Cyrus said. "It takes two whole weeks to make dognip!"

Duchess and Cyrus were sitting next to each other on the grass looking sadly through the opening in the hedge.

"Two whole weeks," Cyrus said again.

Duchess licked Cyrus's face.

"First we've got to get that slipper," Chuck said. Quickly he untied the clothesline and took it down. He made a long loop at the end.

Chuck went through the opening in the hedge and stood at the edge of the neighbor's yard.

"All set," Chuck said and he threw the line.

Chuck has very good aim. The loop landed right on top of the slipper. But, almost at the same moment. Ripper landed on top of the slipper *and* the loop. He grabbed the line in his teeth and ran.

Chuck was so surprised, he dropped the rope he was holding. Ripper ran around and around with Chuck's mother's clothesline in his teeth.

"Don't worry," Will said to Chuck. "If we can get a slipper away from a dog, we can also get a clothesline away from him. Wait a minute!" Will snapped his fingers. "We've got to switch our thinking," he said. "We're on the wrong track. I've got it!"

"Got what?" Chuck sounded miserable.

"Listen," Will said. "The idea is to get the dog away from the slipper—not the slipper away from the dog!"

"How are we going to manage that?" I asked.

"First we should try to distract Ripper," Will said. "Chuck, are there any juicy bones in your house?"

"There are some in a bag in the refrigerator," Chuck said. He didn't sound too hopeful.

"I'll go get them," I said, and I ran inside.

I looked in the refrigerator. There were two paper bags. I immediately felt a bone in one of them. I grabbed the bag and ran outside.

"Now," Will said. "Chuck, you stand at the edge of the yard nearest the slipper. And, Toria, you go around to the opposite side—over there. When I say, 'GO!', Toria, you throw the bone, and Chuck, you run for the slipper."

"Sounds dangerous," I said.

But I did what I was told. I stayed very close to the hedge. Ripper followed me around the yard pulling at the end of his chain. Then he ran back to growl at Chuck.

"Ready, set . . . *GO*!" Will called.

I reached into the bag and threw. Right before the bone left my hand, it occurred to me that there was a lot of meat on it.

Chuck never moved. He never ran for the slipper. He was staring across the yard at the bone lying on the ground.

It *was* a bone. But there was a whole steak attached to that bone.

"I think I took the wrong bag," I said weakly.

Ripper took one sniff at the steak and ran back to snarl at Chuck. He wasn't even interested in steak!

Chuck seemed to be paralyzed. He just stood there looking from the gold slipper to the clothesline to the tennis ball to the nice juicy steak—all lying within reach of Ripper's chain. I ran around the edge of the yard to Chuck. Will was already there.

"Now, take it easy," Will was saying to Chuck. "Things could be worse. We can always wash off the steak; the gold slipper isn't even chewed . . ."

Chuck turned to look at Will. He had a dazed expression on his face.

"The most important thing," Will went on,

"is that we are finally on the right track—"

Chuck exploded. "You and your bright ideas!" he yelled at Will. "We're not on the right track. We're not on any track at all. We're going around in circles!"

At that very second Will and Chuck thought of the solution. We got everything out of the yard. Can you guess how we did it before you turn the page?

A Slipper for Ripper

Will and Chuck's Solution:

Chuck walked around and around the edge of his neighbor's yard. Ripper followed him. As he did, his chain wrapped around and around the tree. It got shorter and shorter.

When Ripper's chain was all wrapped up, he couldn't reach the slipper. We all ran into the yard. Cyrus grabbed the gold slipper; Will got the clothesline; I grabbed the steak; and Duchess got her tennis ball.

Then Chuck walked the other way around. Ripper unwrapped himself.

Chuck's mother never found out!

By the way, Cyrus is not interested in making money out of his secret formula for dognip.

"Besides, what if Mom found out I wore the same socks for two weeks!" he said to me.

The Case of the Haunted Dollhouse

SANDY HARBOR, SUNDAY, MAY 11—

It was the strangest case T*A*C*K ever handled. Things happened so fast I didn't have a chance to write them down at the time. But I will try to recall the events exactly as they took place.

It all started two days ago on Friday morning. I was getting dressed for school when the telephone rang. I ran to answer it.

"Long distance operator calling Toria Gardner."

"This is Toria Gardner," I said.

"Toria," a faint voice said. "It's Abby. I'm calling from a public phone. I didn't want my parents to know. Listen. We're driving down to Sandy Harbor tonight to see Grandma Abigail."

"That's great!" I shouted. Not only is Abigail Pinkwater a special agent of T*A*C*K, she's my best friend in the world.

"Wait a minute." Abby didn't sound very

happy. "Listen to the reason why. My parents are worried about Grandma Abigail. They got a strange letter from her yesterday. They are afraid she is having a nervous breakdown. You see, she's been imagining things—"

"What sort of things?" I asked.

"I don't know!" Abby sounded desperate. "They never tell me anything. They just say things like, 'Let's face it. She's getting old.' "

"But I just saw her last week," I said. "She seemed exactly the same. I took Holly over to her antique shop. She was happy to see us. She gave us ribbon candy the way she always does. Then she showed Holly the Pinkwater Dollhouse."

The Pinkwater Dollhouse is a family heirloom. It has been on display in Grandma Abigail's antique shop ever since I can remember. Children come from all over to see it. It is furnished with tiny antiques.

"That's another thing," Abby said. "In the letter she said she is thinking about selling that dollhouse."

"But she would never do that," I said. "She told me so herself. Her father built it for her when she was a baby. The baby in that little cradle is supposed to be her—" I stopped. Why was I telling Abby about her own grandmother?

"Toria," Abby said. "Something strange is going on . . ." There was a crackling noise on the line. Then the operator said, "Another dollar seventy-five for the next three minutes."

"But I just used up my whole allowance!" Abby said. "Listen, Toria. We won't get there until late tonight. I'll call you first thing tomorrow."

"But Abby—"

Abby didn't hear me. She had already been cut off.

Will and I went right from school to the Pinkwater Mansion. It is a beautiful old house right off Main Street. It is on a hill with a carved stone wall around it. Grandma Abigail's antique shop has always been on the ground floor. She lives on the upper three floors of the old mansion.

When we went in the front gate, I looked up at the sign; ABIGAIL PINKWATER'S LOST AND FOUND.

Underneath it—hanging from it—was another sign.

"Hey!" I said to Will. "That sign wasn't there last week!"

The new sign read, TO THE TRADE ONLY.

"What's that mean?" I asked Will.

"I think it means she will only sell to other antique dealers," Will said. "It's closed to the public."

"But that's crazy," I said. "Grandma Abigail loves the public."

Will and I climbed the stone steps to the front door. On the front door there was another sign. I stared at it. I couldn't believe my eyes. NO CHILDREN, PLEASE.

"What's going on?" I was shocked. "Grandma Abigail loves children. This is ridiculous!"

I pushed the buzzer. Will peeked in the big bay window of the antique shop.

"Someone's watching us," Will said. "He's waving us away."

I looked in the window. "Oh, that's just Mr. Jones, her assistant. He knows who I am." I waved to him and called. "It's me. Toria! Abby's friend, Toria!"

The face disappeared. A second later the door opened.

"My, my. I didn't recognize you," Mr. Jones said. "How you've grown."

I stared at him. "But you just saw me last week."

Mr. Jones laughed. "Children grow so fast." Mr. Jones is a young man, but he wears wire-rimmed glasses that make him look much older. I never cared for him, but Grandma Abigail says he knows more about antiques than anyone she's ever met.

"Well, well," Mr. Jones said. "I'll be sure to tell Mrs. Pinkwater you were here."

"Can't we see her?" Will and I stepped into the enormous front hall.

"She's resting upstairs," Mr. Jones said. "She hasn't been well."

"Wait a minute!" I pointed past him. "The elevator is on its way down. She must be coming down."

Mr. Jones turned around. "Well, well, aren't you lucky?" he said.

The elevator door opened and Grandma Abigail stepped out. It is a tiny old elevator—only big enough for one person. My father told me it was the first elevator in Sandy Harbor.

Grandma Abigail seemed surprised to see us. "Toria! Will! What are you two doing here?"

I looked at her closely to see if she had suddenly become one of those people who detest children. She looked the same.

"We just came for a visit," I said. "And of course we wanted to see the dollhouse. You know how we children love that dollhouse." I poked Will.

"Everyone likes the Pinkwater Dollhouse," Will said stiffly.

Grandma Abigail suddenly looked very tired. "Maybe another time. We had a little accident in the dollhouse a few days ago."

"What happened?" I asked.

"Some china broke," she said. "I—"

Mr. Jones interrupted. "And it just so happened that the Baldwin children were in the shop at the time."

"But those children were nowhere near the dollhouse," Grandma Abigail said. "I saw it happen. The china plates just slipped right off the little shelves and crashed onto the dollhouse floor."

"How awful!" The dollhouse china is real antique china. It was specially made for the dollhouse.

The buzzer rang. Mr. Jones went to the door.

"Ah," he said to a lady customer, "Mrs. Hopewell. We were expecting you. Let me show you that silver vase."

He took Mrs. Hopewell through the doorway that leads into the antique shop.

Grandma Abigail took us each by the hand. "Come, children," she said. "I'll get you some ribbon candy to take with you and maybe you'll come for a longer visit another time."

She took us into the antique shop. The Pinkwater Dollhouse was standing just where it always stands—on a large wooden table against the wall.

We stood in front of the counter while Grandma Abigail took a large glass bowl off a shelf. The bowl was filled with ribbon candy. She reached into the bowl. Suddenly her hand started to tremble. She clutched the ribbon candy in her fist. Her knuckles turned white. Grandma Abigail was crushing the ribbon candy to pieces!

I looked up at her face. She was staring past

me. The expression on her face made chills go up my neck. She was staring at the dollhouse.

Will turned around. I forced myself to turn around too. We took a few steps toward the dollhouse. At first I didn't notice anything wrong.

"It's only the chandelier," I said.

The chandelier in the dollhouse living room was swinging back and forth. That was all.

Then a thought struck me. There was no draft. There was no breeze. *There was no reason for that chandelier to be swinging!*

Will reached out and put his finger on the chandelier. It stopped swinging.

"Don't touch it!" Grandma Abigail called sharply. Then she turned around and called Jones who was on the other side of the shop.

He came over. "What is it?" he asked.

"Jones," she said in a low voice, "I want that dollhouse out of here this evening. Before you leave, I want you to put it up in the attic. On Monday you can call your friend and tell him we accept his offer."

"Whatever you say, Mrs. Pinkwater." Jones looked at us. "Time to go, children."

"But we didn't do anything," I said.

Jones smiled. "I'm sure you didn't," he whispered. "But Mrs. Pinkwater finds children a bit tiring lately."

Grandma Abigail was still staring at the dollhouse. She looked as if she had seen a ghost.

When we got outside, Will said, "I just don't get it. No one was anywhere near the dollhouse. But there's got to be a simple explanation."

"There is," I said.

"What?" Will was surprised.

"The dollhouse is haunted," I said. I had goosebumps all over my arms. "That's why she wants to get rid of it."

Will didn't look scared at all; he just looked puzzled.

My mother invited Will to stay for dinner. Before dinner Will went out to visit my father in his workshed in the backyard. "I just want to see if he's got any new magic tricks," Will said.

My father, Ross Gardner, is an inventor. He works very hard, but he is always glad to see Will and discuss his favorite hobby—magic.

When it was time for dinner, I had to go to the workshed and get them.

I followed them to the house. Popsy had his arm around Will's shoulders.

"Now," Popsy was saying, "you must never

show a child a trick more than once. You see, children see things quicker than grown-ups. Grown-ups see what they expect to see. Children don't. They'll figure it out the second time."

For some reason I thought of the sign on the door of the mansion, NO CHILDREN, PLEASE.

We sat down to dinner. Holly wanted to sit next to Will.

"Speaking of ghosts . . ." my father suddenly said to Will.

"Is that what you were talking to Popsy about?" I asked Will.

"In general," Will said quickly. "We were talking about ghosts and magic *in general.*"

". . . there's an old trick," my father went on. "Wait a minute." He called to my mother, "Dear, do you have an empty bottle with a cork?"

"But Ross," my mother called, "I was just about to take the roast out of the oven."

"It will just take a minute," Popsy said.

"There's an empty bottle out here in the kitchen," my mother called.

Popsy left the room. In a few minutes he was

back. First he lit the candles. Then he turned off the lights. He sat down at the table and set the bottle in front of him.

We looked at the bottle. Hanging down inside the bottle was a string with a gold ring tied to it. The string was attached to the cork.

"Now, we will all hold hands," Popsy said in this eerie voice. "Someone will ask the bottle a question, but, keep in mind, this bottle can only answer yes or no. If the answer is yes, the gold ring will tap the side of the bottle once. If the answer is no, it will tap the side of the bottle twice. Are you ready?"

Will suddenly sat up straight. He seemed very excited. I thought of the swinging chandelier. He must see some connection, I thought.

Will asked the bottle the first question.

"Is the world round?" he asked.

We watched. Then slowly the ring hanging on the string swung to the right and tapped the side of the bottle once.

"How does the bottle know that?" Holly asked. "Please, please, can I ask the next question?"

"Go ahead," my father said in a deep scary voice.

"Will I get a dog for my birthday?" Holly asked.

Once again we watched the gold ring. It swung and tapped the side of the bottle and swung back. Then it tapped the side of the bottle a second time. No.

Holly looked disappointed, but Will burst out laughing. I knew at once he had figured it out.

"As I was saying," my father said. "Never repeat a trick in front of children."

"I know too!" Holly shouted.

The bottle trick gave us the clue to the Mystery of the Swinging Chandelier. But how was it done? Try to guess before you turn this page . . .

The Case of the Haunted Dollhouse

Will and Holly's Solution:

"You see, you just lift the table a tiny bit with your knee and it tilts a little to one side," Popsy explained. "The movement is slight, but it's enough to start the gold ring swinging so that it hits the side of the bottle."

Popsy turned on the lights. "Another way to perform that trick is by stepping on a loose floorboard under one of the legs of the table," he added.

Will kicked me under the table. "Did you hear that, Toria? A loose floorboard."

After dinner, I said to Will, "So you think that's how it happened? Wait until Grandma Abigail hears it was just a loose floorboard. Anyone could have stepped on it by mistake and started the chandelier swinging."

"It explains the china slipping off the shelf too," Will said. "First thing tomorrow, we'll go over there and clear up this whole thing."

The Case of the Haunted Dollhouse Part II

SAME TIME, SAME PLACE–

It wasn't over yet.

As I said before, it was the strangest case T*A*C*K ever handled.

It was also the most dangerous.

Early the next morning Will and I went to the Pinkwater Mansion. We couldn't wait to explain the mystery and show everyone how simple it all was.

No one answered the door. We looked up at the house. All the curtains were closed. And Abby's car was nowhere to be seen.

"What's going on?" I asked. "Nobody's here!"

"I had a feeling we should have come over last night," Will said.

There was nothing we could do. The house was completely closed up. We went back to my house and waited. "I'm sure Abby will call," I kept saying. I felt very nervous.

Late in the afternoon I saw Abby coming up the walk. I ran to the door and hugged her.

Abby looked terrible. She had dark circles under her eyes. She came into the living room and flopped down in a chair.

"Abby!" Will said. "What happened? Did you just arrive?"

"No, we arrived late last night. But, when we got there, Grandma had already gone. The house was locked up. We went to a phone and called all her friends. We finally found her at your Aunt Christobel's."

"Is that where you are staying?" Will asked her.

Abby nodded.

"Is your grandmother all right?" I asked. "What made her leave her own house?"

Abby lowered her voice. "She said . . ." Abby looked around. "Is anyone here?" she asked. "I don't want anyone to hear this."

"Don't worry," I said. "Popsy's in his workshed and Mom's taken Holly to buy new shoes."

Abby spoke in a whisper anyway. "Grandma Abigail said she had to leave because of the ghost in the dollhouse!"

"But there *is* no ghost," I said. "Listen. . . ."

Will and I told Abby the whole story. ". . . it was just a loose floorboard. That explains the whole thing!"

Abby listened. She had a funny look on her face. "That's very nice," she said. "But it was a different ghost that scared her out of that house—an *altogether different ghost*!"

Will and I stared at Abby.

"Look," she said. "Everyone is saying that Grandma Abigail is completely off her head. And that scares me more than anything else." Abby took a deep breath. "You see, it wasn't the first time she heard sounds coming from that dollhouse—"

"Sounds?" Will asked.

"Yes. Last Friday night—a week ago—she said she suddenly woke up in the middle of the night. She was freezing cold. The temperature in the house had dropped. She heard piano music coming from somewhere. She put on her robe and took the elevator to the first floor. The music was coming from the dollhouse. It was a song her father used to play—" Abby stopped. She had tears in her eyes.

"Then what?" Will asked softly.

"Then she called your Aunt Christobel, who

told her to be sensible and go back to sleep. She said it was just a bad dream."

"Sounds like Aunt Christobel," Will said. "But what happened last night?"

"Last night—" Abby covered her face with her hands. "Oh it's so awful!"

I went over and put my arm around her. We waited for Abby to go on.

"Last night," she said, "Grandma Abigail was making herself some tea when all at once the house got very cold again. The temperature had dropped—"

"That's it!" I suddenly shouted. "The temperature dropped! It always drops when a ghost comes around. You see, Abby, you have nothing to worry about. Your grandmother isn't the least bit crazy. It's just a real live ghost!"

Will and Abby were staring at me. I wasn't sure I had said the right thing. "Go on," I whispered. "I didn't mean to interrupt."

"This time," Abby went on, "she heard a baby crying—very softly. The sound seemed to be coming from the attic. She went up to the attic. The baby's cries got louder. They were coming from the dollhouse which Jones had put in the attic. The little cradle was turned on its side and the baby was lying on the floor of the dollhouse. Then the sound stopped."

"What did she do?" I asked hoarsely.

"She called Will's Aunt Christobel and said she was coming right over—that she was never going back home. Then she packed her bag and closed down the house."

Will got up and went to sit on the window sill. He didn't say anything for a while. Then he asked, "Did anyone call the police?"

"Christobel did, but she said she felt like a fool. And she said she didn't like everyone in Sandy Harbor knowing Grandma Abigail was loony. She was sure Sergeant Small was laughing at her when she told him the story. He said he didn't have many complaints about haunted dollhouses, but he said he'd send someone around sometime next week to look the place over." A tear rolled down Abby's cheek.

"Next week will be too late," Will muttered. He was gazing out the window. "You know," he said. "There's another reason for the temperature to drop."

"What's that?" I asked.

"The furnace went off," Will said.

"Don't be ridiculous, Will," I said.

"Wait a minute!" Will jumped to his feet. "I think I can explain the temperature and those sounds too!" He turned sharply to Abby.

"Abby," Will said, "can you get us into that house?"

"Now?" Abby asked.

Will nodded.

"But it's all locked up," Abby said.

"Abby," Will said in a very gentle voice. "If you can get us into that house, I will prove to you that your grandmother is perfectly sane and that there are no ghosts!"

Abby looked at Will for a few seconds. Then she said, "Well, there is that door under the back porch. It leads into the cellar. We could see . . ."

Before I knew it, we were standing at the gate to the Pinkwater Mansion. I didn't like this adventure one bit, but Abby happens to be my best friend. I couldn't let her down.

To make matters worse, I heard thunder. Then I saw a flash of lightning.

"It's going to pour," I said.

"We'll be dry once we're inside," Will said. There was another streak of lightning.

"Oh, boy," I muttered. "Just like a haunted house movie." But I followed them around to the back porch.

We crawled through some wooden slats and under the back porch. The door to the cellar had a metal latch. Will lifted the latch and pulled the door open.

I was the last one in. I pulled the door shut behind me. Then I heard the latch fall back into place.

"Oh no!" I called to the others. "Now I've done it! We're locked in." It was so dark I couldn't see anyone else. "How will we get out again?"

"Don't worry," Will called. "Later on we can always climb out through that window."

I looked up. The window was up high. It didn't look easy to open. I bumped into a piece of furniture.

"Abby," I heard Will say, "do you know where the master switch is? I want to turn on the electricity."

"It's near the fuse box," Abby said. "On the wall to your right. You'll find a lever."

Will must have pulled it because right away

the cellar light went on. So did a light in the elevator.

The cellar was full of antique furniture and mirrors. I saw Will go over to an old furnace in the corner. He looked behind it.

"I was right!" he said. "There's a tape recorder here!"

I had no idea why Will expected to find a tape recorder behind a furnace, but I said, "Good. I guess we can go home."

"No, Toria," Will said. "We've got to test it to see if the sound from it travels upstairs. Now, you and Abby go up to the first floor. On the wall where that dollhouse was standing before Jones moved it, you'll find a small opening in the wall with a grate over it. It's a heating duct. Tap three times on the grate and wait—"

Abby was already pulling me over to the elevator.

"Can't we take the stairs?" I asked.

Abby shook her head. "The door at the top of the stairs is always locked from the other side."

As we squeezed into the tiny elevator, Will suddenly said, "Wait! You'll need this." He reached into his back pocket and handed Abby a small flashlight. Then he went back to the furnace and opened the furnace door.

The elevator door closed. Slowly it moved up to the first floor. We got out of the elevator and went into the antique shop. It wasn't so dark in there. I walked quickly. "Let's get this over with," I said.

I found the grate Will was talking about and tapped three times. A few seconds later we heard old-fashioned piano music coming from the grate.

"Now I get it!" Abby said. "The sound from the tape recorder travels up from the furnace and through the heating ducts."

I felt much braver. I felt sure that, in the end, everything was going to be explained.

Then I heard my name. "Toria," a faint voice called. I clutched Abby's arm.

"Don't be scared," Abby said. "It's just Will talking through the duct."

"Toria," the voice said again. "Check where the loose floorboard is. I just want to know which one of us could have stepped on it yesterday."

I found the board under one of the table legs.

I looked along the length of it. Then I walked along it. It wiggled a little when I came to the table with the silver vase.

I went back to the grate and called, "It was either Mr. Jones or that lady."

"Good work, Toria," the faint voice said.

I felt very efficient.

"Now," Will said. "Go to the attic and see if there's another grate behind that dollhouse."

"I don't mind," I said to Abby. "This is kind of interesting."

"Very interesting," Abby said, and we took the elevator to the attic.

When the door opened, the attic was pitch-dark. Abby shined the little flashlight around.

"Be careful," she told me.

I took a tiny step. Then another. I pulled my foot back. "Hey!" I said. "There's nothing under my foot. I almost fell through."

"It's the trapdoor," Abby said. "I wonder why it's open." I held the flashlight while Abby tugged at the trapdoor. It banged shut.

She took the flashlight again and shined it on the dollhouse. "Tap on the grate," she said to me.

I tapped. A few seconds later a baby began to cry.

"It's a different duct," Abby said. "You can send the sound to different parts of the house through the heating system."

"Well, that's very clever," I said. "But who would play a joke like this on Grandma Abigail?"

"It isn't a joke," Abby said.

She shined the flashlight around the attic. She held the beam of light on some velvet drapes that covered the window. Suddenly the flashlight went off.

"What happened?" I asked. "Why did the flashlight go out?"

"I turned it out," Abby said. Her voice was very calm and cool. "Go to the elevator, Toria," she said. "We are leaving right this minute. Don't ask me any questions."

Abby and I backed away toward the elevator. I pushed the button. The door opened and we got in. Abby pushed the button for the basement. It took a few seconds for the door to close.

We were moving.

"Please hurry," Abby whispered to the elevator.

"What's the matter, Abby?" I asked. "What did you see?"

Abby didn't answer. She was leaning against the elevator wall. Her eyes were closed.

"What was it!" I was scared to death.

The elevator door opened to the cellar. Will was standing there.

"We're leaving right now," Abby said to Will, and she ran to the cellar door.

"Abby!" I screamed. "I told you it was locked!"

Abby kept pounding on it. "It can't be," she panted.

She stopped pounding and ran back.

"Look, we've got to get out of here. We've got to get the police," she said.

All of a sudden the elevator started moving again. It was going up. I looked at the numbers above the elevator . . . first floor . . . second floor . . .

"A ghost riding an elevator?" I asked.

"Not a ghost," Abby said. "Jones! Jones was hiding behind those curtains. I saw his eyes behind those wire glasses!"

The elevator stopped on the attic floor.

I looked around desperately. "The cellar door is locked. The door at the top of the stairs is locked. *We've got to get out that window!"*

"No, Toria." Will grabbed my arm. "There's not enough time for all of us to get out. We need time."

The elevator was on its way down. Third floor . . . second floor . . .

"He's coming to get us," Abby whispered. "We've got to hide!"

"Hold it!" Will suddenly said. "We don't have to. I know what we can do!"

Will got us into this mess. But he also got us out of it again. Do you know how?

The Case of the Haunted Dollhouse Part II

Will's Solution:

Will waited a second. Then he pulled the master switch and turned off all the electricity in the house. Everything—including the elevator—went out. Jones was stuck between floors!

It took us almost fifteen minutes to get out of that cellar. The window was stuck, so we had to take the hinges off the cellar door and go out that way.

We ran to a neighbor and called the police. They came and arrested Jones.

As it turned out, Jones had been cheating Grandma Abigail for years. This time he had had an offer for $150,000 for the Pinkwater Dollhouse; he was only planning to pay Grandma Abigail $30,000 of it. He was going to keep the rest. He had haunted the dollhouse to get Grandma Abigail to sell it.

Grandma Abigail was perfectly fine after it was over. But she scolded us for hours for "taking chances."